HÄ[GAR]
THE HORRIBLE

VIKINGS ARE FUN

by Dik Browne

Volume I of
THE BEST OF HAGAR THE HORRIBLE

TOR
A TOM DOHERTY ASSOCIATES BOOK

HAGAR THE HORRIBLE: VIKINGS ARE FUN

Copyright © 1982, 1988 by King Features Syndicate, Inc.

A TOR Book
Published by Tom Doherty Associates, Inc.
49 West 24 Street
New York, NY 10010

ISBN: 0-812-56762-5   Can. ISBN: 0-812-56763-3

First edition: February 1983

Printed in the United States of America

0   9   8   7   6   5

ROCK STORY

THE DEBATE

NEIGHBORS

THE BOSS

TIME OUT

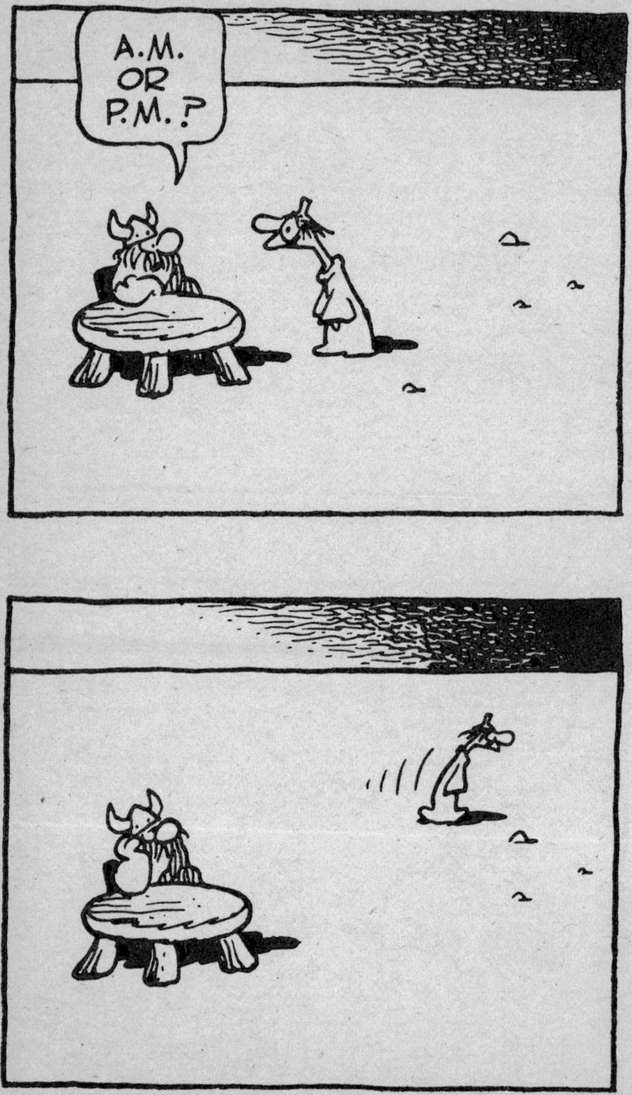
A.M. OR P.M.?

FOOLHARDY
HOW DO I GET TO BE A VIKING?
FIRST YOU GOTTA DO SOMETHING INCREDIBLY BRAVE!

BAD NEWS

WISDOM

WHAT ARE YOU THINKING ABOUT, HAMLET, MY SON?

I'M THINKING THE MOON LOOKS SMALLER BECAUSE THE SHADOW OF THE EARTH IS ON IT...

HO-HE...THE SHADOW OF THE EARTH!!

DON'T SNICKER, STUPID! EXPLAIN MOON TO THE POOR CHILD!

FEARLESS

NO JOKE

NEAT TRICK

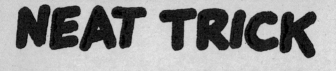

THE LESSON

NOSTALGIA

LUNCH

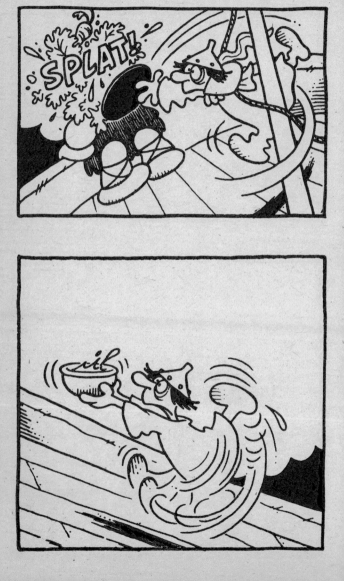

SOME BOOTY

WHAT IS IT?
WATCH _

THAT'S FUNNY... WHEN I TURNED IT ON IN THE PALACE, WATER CAME OUT

TIDY TIME

OH, THOSE

SAILORS

FACTS

MOTHERLY

ADVICE

FATHERLY

PRIDE

AND LOOK WHERE YOU'RE GOING! DO YOU WANT TO BREAK MY NECK?
WATCH OUT FOR THAT HOLE, YOU MORON!

SWEET

DREAMS

HOME RULE

DO IT

STORY

"QUICKLY I GRABBED IT— AND IT WAS A TINY MAGIC TROLL.

"AND HE SAID IF I LET HIM GO...

"HE'D GRANT ME ANY THREE WISHES — AND SO I DID!"

REALLY?!! I CAN'T BELIEVE IT!
I BELIEVE IT!

WHAT WAS YOUR THIRD WISH?
A BAG OF PEANUTS.

DAWN

ODD JOB

BOP!

I'M BREAKING
THEM IN
FOR HAGAR.

ORDER